Ron Mueller

&ropdfLittle Otter & Talking Wren ℰℬ

By: *Ron Mueller*

Around the World Publishing LLC
Cincinnati, Ohio

ISBN 13: 978-1-68223-419-8

Distribution By: Ingram
Cover Design: By: Ron Mueller
Cover Picture By: Hien Mueller

Ron Mueller

Dedicated to the odd but lifelong couple

Ron Mueller

Little Otter and Talking Wren

*T*alking Wren had informed her parents of her desire to be part of the long hunt team. They at first questioned her desire but they knew that her two friends had chosen to be on the hunt team. Talking Wren listened as each of her parents gave their version of approval.

Her mother focused on being careful and being safe.

Her father spent time with giving her hunting tips and showing her how to use a spear.

He was Impressed when she showed him the spear made by Taelo, Golden Hawk and Burley Bear. He commented on both its good balance, the quality of the wood and its beauty. He said that such attention to detail and the fact that the three were looking out for her was a good sign.

His comments seemed to help her mother accept the hunting arrangement. Her mother gave her a large sleeping hide and a soft covering hide to keep her warm.

Talking Wren knew that it was her way of saying she thought it would be a great opportunity for her daughter.

1

She knew immediately that it was going to be a good long hunt when Taelo suggested to Little Otter that Burley Bear lead the way to the Cave of the Other because he had to pick up a few critical hunting items.

She suspected that a change from the crappy hunting ground area they had been assigned was going to happen.

The cave of the Others impressed and overwhelmed Talking Wren. It was massive, spacious, and blessed with an amazing panoramic view.

Her mind immediately began to analyze the layout and the well-organized arrangement of the living quarters and the gathering area. She went to the warm water pool and dipped her hand in. She stood looking out at the long-lush valley beyond the pool. It was clear to her that the Others had a home that would be wanted by everyone. She envied the clans good fortune.

She had heard the story of how Taelo had found the cave and it came to her as she turned slowly around to take it all in.

He had been led to it by a large male elk.

The eagle had cried out from above.

She wished the animals talked to her as they did to Taelo.

She thought about the hard winter they had just lived through and imagined what it would have been like if every day she could have bathed in the warm water pool. She envied the luxury enjoyed by the Others.

No wonder the entire clan had been out on the beach to greet Taelo.

She saw Taelo and the person she had learned was Broken Spear, the Seer of the Others lead the way into the pool, she followed the rest of the team and sat down on boulders that had been placed beneath the water.

The water was up to her shoulders. She closed her eyes and let the heat warm her.

Later, after the team set up their sleeping area, she was seated on a convenient boulder and eating a very well-prepared buffalo meat dinner that was flavored in an unusual but very tasty way. She was listening to Taelo, Golden Hawk and Broken Spear discuss the upcoming hunt.

She was caught by surprise when Broken Spear commented about having Meadow Flower, Burley Bear's future mate, join the long hunt team so that he would not be the only one that was not paired with a future mate.

Meadow Flower looked at each of the male Elk Clan members. Taelo and Golden Hawk were already the target of her two friends, Quiet Rabbit and Busy Bee.

That left Little Otter for her.

She had long ago decided that his name was misleading. He was a large powerful person at least three times her size.

She wondered whether the Seer was mistaken in his assessment of the team.

She almost fell off her boulder, when Broken Spear looked over at her and gave her a wink and a nod.

She found it hard to swallow when he went on to comment that the long hunt experience would bond them all for life.

She looked again at Little Otter. She decided that he was very large, but he was just as handsome as Taelo or Golden Hawk. She would see if he had other redeeming qualities.

This was a situation that she had not imagined.

Little Otter had taken in the discussion and wondered which of the three women on the hunt team was the one meant for him. He was confident in himself but extremely shy and had not even thought about hunting with a potential mate.

The discussion disturbed him, and he decided that he would let the leaves blow as they may.

He knew he had been selected to lead the long hunt only because a few of the leaders objected to Taelo or Golden Hawk as the leaders.

The objection was actually about having women on the hunt team, but the objectors did not want to challenge Taelo's mother, White Swan. They had come to recognize that she was astute at managing the politics of the Elk Clan.

Little Otter was pleased to have been the third person selected. He had not expected to have been considered to hunt with the likes of the other three male hunters on the team. He had observed their capabilities and knew his hunting skills were a distant fourth behind.

Little Otter and Talking Wren

As they left the Clan of Others and Burley Bear led the team in a new direction, Little Otter realized he was in charge in name only. He had no idea where they would hunt. He wondered if he had lost his leadership position.

Taelo, Golden Hawk and Burley Bear had agreed to hunt in a more abundant location than the desert area originally designated to the team.

They had agreed to give one third of their take to the Clan of Others and to share all the buffalo that the Others could hunt from the Valley of Plenty.

Little Otter was pleased to be hunting in a more promising region. He had not especially liked the attitude of the leaders that had told him that little was expected of his team and he should just concentrate in keeping the women safe.

When they arrived at the site suggested by Broken Spear, Taelo announced that Little Otter should organize the team and prepare for the hunt.

He was pleased that Taelo was not taking over the leadership role. He stepped forward and announced that teams would be organized based on the speed of each member.

He stated that he knew Taelo, and Golden Hawk were the two fastest. They would each lead a hunt team.

He had no idea about the women and had decided on a race to see how to place each of them. He explained that the fastest would be placed with Taelo, the second fastest with Golden Hawk, the third fastest with Burley Bear and the slowest with him.

The outcome was very clear. Quiet Rabbit seemed to fly past all the others. Busy Bee was a distant second just ahead of Talking Wren who seemed not be trying to beat her two friends.

He knew Meadow Flower, would be last. The Others were powerful but not built for speed.

He had planned to put the third fastest woman with Burley Bear. He figured it would be Talking Wren.

Taelo, had casually commented that clear communication between partners was very important.

He was not fluent in the language of the Others and knew that Meadow Flower had limited understanding of his language.

This caused him to change Meadow Flower from supporting Golden Hawk to pairing her with Burley Bear.

He reassigned Talking Wren to be his hunt partner.

Talking Wren thought back through the race. When the race had started, she had taken the lead and stayed in front out to the marker tree.

As she went around it, she was passed by Busy Bee.

Then Quiet Rabbit surprised her by passing them both and stretching her lead by at least three spears lengths.

It was clear to her that Quiet Rabbit had dug deep for all the speed she could muster.

She had thought about passing Busy Bee but decided against it because she realized that Busy Bee wanted to hunt with Golden Hawk.

She relaxed and took third.

The outcome was very clear.

She was surprised when Little Otter changed the hunt pair assignments. His logic about needing clear communication between hunt partners made sense and she readily accepted working with him.

The hunt began immediately after having been paired. She and Little Otter followed Golden Hawk and Busy Bee. They listened to his hunt instructions to Busy Bee.

She quickly realized that Busy Bee would need to carry two spears and keep up with Golden Hawk as he raced forward carrying an additional two spears.

He said that he was targeting four buffalo.

Talking Wren clearly understood that Golden Hawk was planning on at least three buffalo with a fourth one if he was fast enough.

She commented that she and Little Otter would do their part.

Talking Wren turned to Little Otter and asked if downing four buffalo as described by Golden Hawk was possible?

Little Otter replied that he thought Golden Hawk was exaggerating and that if they got one buffalo between the two teams, they would be lucky.

Golden Hawk dropped back and joined the two as they jogged out toward the herd. He explained how the two should ensure each animal was dead and then gut them and prepare them to be hauled into the forest where they would be hung up and processed.

She then remembered Burley Bear's story about watching Taelo and Golden Hawk take down the three buffalo they had brought back on the sled that pulled to the Elk Clan.

Then the hunt began.

Talking Wren was impressed at Golden Hawk's ability to cull out four young buffalo and get them moving toward the forest. When Golden Hawk began the run, she and Little Otter followed as closely as possible, but they could not keep up.

She kept looking ahead as the first two buffalo dropped to their knees. They were dead.

Golden Hawk did not stop.

She watched as Busy Bee sped up to hand him the next spear.

He ran out ahead and downed the third buffalo.

She wondered how Busy Bee had been able to keep up as she hand Golden Hawk the fourth spear.

What blew her mind was Golden Hawk's ability to accelerate, pass and plant the spear for the fourth buffalo to skewer itself.

She thought he had been running at top speed. Then, he left Busy Bee behind and pulled ahead of the fourth buffalo and plant the spear.

She and Little Otter found each buffalo dead and in the same front kneeling position with a spear deeply imbedded between its front legs.

She was sure each spear had gone through the heart.

She looked back to where Taelo's team had hunted and saw them pulling a buffalo into the woods. She wondered how many buffalo they had taken down.

She thought of renaming him Talking Otter as she listened to Little Otter go on and on about his team killing four buffalo. He urged Taelo and his team to help Golden Hawk and his team. "After all they had killed four ..four buffalo."

She watched as Taelo and Burly Bear pulled one of their team's kill into the woods.

Later, by her count she realized that Taelo's team had also killed four and were processing their last buffalo. She wondered how they could have done it so fast.

Her team was still processing their second one.

As she watched Burley Bear and Meadow flower and how fast they were at skinning their last animal she understood how Taelo's team had been so fast to hang their kill. She and Little Otter were snails in comparison to them.

She watched as Taelo and Quiet Rabbit went out to the herd. She did not get a satisfying answer from Burley Bear when she asked what Taelo was doing.

He said something about an out of season young calf.

She joined the other members of the team as they stood at the edge of the forest to see what Taelo was up to. She realized how good he was at staying out of sight. She could see the mother buffalo slowly move away from the main herd and come towards the woods, but she could not see either Taelo or Quiet Rabbit.

Taelo was much closer to the Buffalo than Talking Wren expected. His take down of the rather large calf was swift and effective.

Then Talking Wren drew a deep breath as Quite Rabbit jumped up to block the mother buffalo. She could not help but yell encouragement to her friend. She was pleased that the rest of the team joined her on her second yell.

Meadow Flower commented that they did not have to worry about Quiet Rabbit. Quiet Rabbit had repeatedly demonstrated her bravery and now she was armed with yet another skill.

Had the mother buffalo charged Quiet Rabbit would have used that skill to plant the spear and kill her.

By late afternoon, Talking Wren walked alongside the travois being pulled by the young but large buffalo. The travois was loaded with an entire buffalo carcass.

This was a very strange experience. She was not sure how to take it in.

She asked Taelo several times how he had figured out that the young bull would pull the travois.

Taelo's response had been that the memory of he, Golden Hawk and Burly Bear pulling the sled with three buffalo from the valley of plenty and up the beach to the Elk Clan's camp had inspired him to think about getting someone or something else to pull the travois.

He jokingly commented that it was either the bull or the three women on the team that he had chosen for the chore.

He said he had been so afraid of the second choice that he had taken the huge risk with the young bull.

The power of the young buffalo gave Talking Wren a lesson in applying one's observation and to extend that learning to something beyond what she knew.

She likened it to Taelo extrapolating a small river fish catching trap to an extremely large one that fit the scale of the cove and the ocean.

She was aware that Taelo had come up with the fish trap by watching how a group of adults guided the spent salmon to the edge of the river before picking them up and taking them to shore.

Now he had thought through the act of pulling the heavy sled and extended this to having an animal do it.

She commented that he had been wise to choose the young buffalo to pull the travois.

He smiled at her and said that the young bull had been sent to him by the Ancestors who had communicated the same sentiment that he should choose wisely.

He said he had taken the easier path with the young bull.

She promised herself that she would figure out how to do something similar.

When Little Otter volunteered to take the first load of meat to the Clan of the Others and then onto the Elk Clan, she volunteered to be his travel partner.

She would have preferred to have stayed to hunt with the rest of the team but chose to support her hunt partner.

She figured it might give them some time to learn more about each other.

She was surprised at the speed and distance they could travel during each sun cycle. Had they been pulling the heavy load they would have been exhausted after each sun cycle. Instead, they were able to enjoy a well-cooked evening meal.

The nights were getting increasingly colder, and she found that sleeping next to Little Otter was like sleeping next to a warming fire.

She smiled as she thought about such an arrangement.

He was a good listener and gave her complements on everything she prepared on the cooking fire.

He was also a much deeper thinker than she had given him credit. He was constantly posing questions that required her to stop and think before replying.

His questions seemed to open knew thought paths for her.

Talking Wren gained a deeper understanding of her hunt partner and became less concerned about Broken Spear's prediction of mates hunting together.

Broken Spear's and the Clan of Others' greetings, and a welcome dinner put Talking Wren at ease.

She talked with Broken Spear as they ate dinner.

She listened carefully as he explained that Taelo would face a life-threatening experience while she and Little Otter were away.

The journey down the coast toward the Elk Clan cove was serene. The coastal wind was at their back and the sun was to their front.

Little Otter and the young buffalo seemed to have formed a strong and smooth working relationship. Their steady pace took them to their destination in just three sun cycles.

Talking Wren kept her feet dry, but she walked along the edge of the sea and collected any unique seashell or other objects that she could later use to decorate the clothes she would make. Occasionally she would find a unique object that she would use to make something unique.

Little Otter found the young buffalo comforting. It seemed to have bonded with him and responded positively to being brushed and occasionally fed grasses and some ground roots.

He listened to Talking Wren's chatter and found it interesting as she went from the analysis of the wind's interaction with the waves, to the reason the moon's appearance changed throughout the seasons, to how she would use some found object to decorate a jacket she planned to make. It was clear to him that her mind was moving about in an almost random fashion trying to analyze the world around her.

He was impressed with the range of thoughts that seemed to flow unstopped from brain to tongue and out into the world.

He was pleased to learn that his team was the first to send back a significant amount of meat. He consciously avoided telling the leaders, that had sent his team to the worst hunting grounds, that his team was not hunting where they had been sent.

He instead let them know that his team's long hunt had just begun.

To his parents and to White Swan, Quiet Pheasant and Floating Cloud he shared that he was learning more than he had ever known about hunting and about what it meant to lead.

He complemented the skill and bravery of the young women on the team.

Talking Wren was impressed with Little Otter's comments and the maturity that it signified.

The trip back, with no load, went at the jogging pace they could maintain. The young bull carried all their load on its back.

Little Otter and Talking Wren

During their travel, Talking Wren brought up the life-threatening experience that Taelo might have had. She wondered what that might have been.

Little Otter's practical reply that they would know when they returned to the camp site was not very satisfying, but it was irrefutable.

When she entered the camp, she was immediately drawn to a huge, stretched hide that Talking Wren learned was a saber tooth tiger. It was as large as the hide of a buffalo. She stood before it and asked how the team had killed it.

She looked at Taelo when she learned that he alone had killed it. She was not expecting an answer when she asked how that was possible. Then she went on to ask about how it had all come about.

Burley Bear stood up and told the tale of the tiger making the mistake of climbing out on the limb where Taelo was asleep. He told how Taelo had pushed the tiger off the limb and then chased after it. He held up two very long saber teeth. He went on to say that when Taelo caught up with the saber tooth tiger he attacked her and grabbed the two teeth and pulled them out as the tigress roared in pain. He then used her own teeth to kill her.

He went on to describe Taelo's egotistical, superior attitude when he had insisted the rest of the team carry the huge carcass back to camp. He then had them skin the beast and prepare the hide to make him a future victory outfit.

With a small smile he insisted that every word he had just spoken was true.

Both Talking Wren and Little Otter chuckled and then joined the rest of the team in congratulating him on his good story telling.

Talking Wren was happy to be back with the team. She then noticed that Quiet Rabbit and Meadow Flower were not in the camp.

Her inquiry about Quiet Rabbit drew out the real story of the crazed tigress and her attacks on the hunt team of the Others and then the attack on Taelo.

She was not surprised at Quiet Rabbit's bravery at chasing after the crazed tigress that was chasing Taelo.

Nor was she surprised by Quiet Rabbits ability to attend to the severe injuries of the wounded hunter.

She was well aware of her friend's quiet intensity, her focused nature and her ability to use her many skills.

She gave Little Otter a hug and commented that his sleeping area had been on the same limb as Taelo's, and the tigress passed by it on the way out to where Taelo slept.

She commented that had he been here he would have had to pull the teeth out and kill her with them because he would not have been able to run as fast or as far as Taelo.

She went on to add that she was not as brave as Quiet Rabbit and would have just yelled words of encouragement down to him from her place up in the tree.

Little Otter smiled and commented that he had thought ahead, and he had volunteered to take the meat to the two clans in the anticipation of just such an incident.

He went on to say that he had been designated as the leader for his ability to think ahead and this incident demonstrated his superior capability.

The next morning Talking Wren watched as Taelo made the stone marker that pointed the direction in which the team would move.

She asked about the drawings of a mastodon in the dirt in the direction the rocks pointed.

Taelo explained that he and Golden Hawk had spotted a large herd traveling slowly southward along the valley where they had hunted the buffalo. He wanted to keep them in sight but said he had no intentions of hunting them until Meadow Flower and Quiet Rabbit rejoined the team.

Talking Wren discussed this with Little Otter. He let her know that Taelo, Golden Hawk and Burley Bear had shared this information with him and that he was in agreement.

Talking Wren began seeing the mate she had been looking for. She also revisited all the words that Broken Spear had spoken to her. One phrase he had shared with her became central.

"You must stand behind your mate and be ready. If you do, you will have a long and prosperous time together."

She was not sure what that meant but she would stay alert and pay attention to her surroundings.

The slow movement of the mix of buffalo and Mastodons allowed the team the luxury of hunting the smaller game like elk, deer, a few boars and the smaller game like rabbits and squirrels.

Talking Wren enjoyed her time hunting with her sling. She and Busy Bee competed on how many rabbits each could bag. She noted that Busy Bee had moved from being the ham-handed slinger to a deadly accurate slinger.

She commented on the change. Busy Bee smiled and replied that she had received hands on training from an expert.

Talking Wren knew better than to pursue the meaning of that comment.

She noticed the pine tree forest thin out. The small game changed in proportion. There were fewer ground hogs and more rabbits. The terrain was covered with more protruding rocks.

She commented on this and learned that the original hunt area that had been assigned to them was farther to the east and even more sparse than the area they were now entering.

Late in the afternoon she saw two people approaching that she knew could only be Quiet Rabbit and Meadow Flower. The two made an odd pair. They were both about the same height, but she compared Quiet Rabbit to a thin willow pole and Meadow Flower to a wide strong oak.

As she called out to the rest of the team, she noted that Burley Bear was already arranging a cooking fire ring and had several cuts of meat on a skewer.

It was clear to her that he had observed the two long before she had.

The Other's had eyesight that was much better than those of the Elk Clan.

She greeted the two as they arrived and immediately reassured Quiet Rabbit that Taelo and Golden Hawk were not hunting mastodons.

She listened as Busy Bee made the point that Taelo had wanted the whole team to participate in what he was calling a once in a lifetime hunt experience that should be shared.

She watched as Taelo, Golden Hawk and Little Otter returned. Each was carrying a portion of what she thought would be a young boar.

Taelo greeted Quiet Rabbit and gave her a hug. He went on to ask how Rolling Stone was doing.

Meadow Flower replied that he was now in the good hands of her sister, Marigold. She assured the team that Marigold would give him the best care anyone could possibly get.

She also let the team know that Broken Spear had renamed Rolling Stone and he was now Saber Scar.

Everyone on the team agreed that the name was appropriate.

He would carry a set of five scars across his chest put there by the mad saber tooth tigress.

Talking Wren was amazed as she listened to Meadow Flower describe how Quiet Rabbit had cleaned the wounds and sutured the five long slashes. She had lost count of the stitches and she joked that Saber Scar now owed Quiet Rabbit a year's supply of honey for the honey Quiet Rabbit used to put in his wound.

The conversation shifted to the up-coming mammoth hunt. She was very interested and listened intently as Taelo explained how the team would hunt the Mastodon.

He explained that it was not a matter of speed, or a matter of attacking the animal.

This animal was so big that their team did not have enough members for an open terrain confrontation. The hunt was more of a trapping effort. He reminded everyone of the fish trap. The fish swam in and then could not swim out.

Talking Wren closed her eyes as she listened. It was clear to her that Taelo had figured out some way to trap the mastodon.

When Taelo described the need for a tight crevasse with sides that were wide at the opening and then narrowed as it reached its end, she immediately understood how the team would kill the animal.

At sunrise she helped clean up their campsite. She was eager to catch up to the mastodon herd.

She had watched Golden Hawk, Taelo and Quiet Rabbit as they jogged ahead to find a place where the trap could be set.

Her goal was to have the team as close to the herd as possible so they would be able to help.

Burley Bear commented that his clan had hunted the mastodon, but their technique had been to run the animal over a cliff. He said that it often resulted in killing more animals than was needed.

Talking Wren agreed that it would be difficult to control a herd of mastodon that had been driven toward a cliff.

She wondered how Taelo would be able to get one mastodon to move away from the herd and into a crevasse. She recalled his skill, when he had culled out the mother buffalo and her calf. She envisioned him doing something similar with a young mammoth.

Quiet Rabbit's return as the sun set was frustrating to Talking Wren. She had trouble sleeping, she wanted to be where the action would take place.

At sunrise she was pushing everyone to get moving. She, Quiet Rabbit and Busy Bee jogged out ahead of the rest. She knew that Quiet Rabbit was concerned that Taelo and Golden Hawk would act before the team got to where they were.

She expressed confidence that Taelo and Golden Hawk would act sensibly.

The crevasse was immediately obvious to Talking Wren. She took in the inward pointing poles. It was a fish trap extrapolated to be applied to a mastodon.

She led the way up along the top side of the crevasse to where it turned, and she could see the young mastodon trapped by the pointed poles behind him. She waved to Taelo and Golden Hawk who were sitting in front of the trapped animal.

Taelo apologized for having guided the mastodon into the crevasse before the team arrived. It had been a matter of timing of the passing herd.

He explained the preparation. He and Golden Hawk had prepared two handful of poles by burning the ends in the fire and creating the sharp points.

They had watched the herd passing by and realized that they would have to guide one mastodon at the edge of the herd toward the crevasse.

They had culled the last young mastodon and slowly moved him toward the crevasse. Once the animal was at the entrance, he and Golden Hawk had stood up waving two hides attached to long poles and yelling to get the mastodon to run into the ravine. They then planted six poles with their points very near to the mastodon's rear. Each time he back up the poles poked him, and he moved farther into the ravine.

The young mastodon that was currently trapped had just reached the end.

Taelo asked if the team was ready to send the mastodon to the land of the ancestors.

The team were eager and said so.

Little Otter and Talking Wren

Talking Wren looked up in surprise as Taelo asked Burley Bear and Little Otter to be the two to drive spears into the mastodon.

She was immediately on the alert.

Broken Spears words, "you must stand behind your mate," thundered through her mind as Taelo positioned Burley Bear and then asked Meadow Flower to stand behind him.

He looked up and seemed to look at her.

A shiver ran down her spine as she immediately took a position behind Little Otter.

Taelo asked if everyone was ready.

Talking Wren took in the team. Burley Bear and Meadow Flower were directly across from Little Otter and her. Quiet Rabbit was standing next to Taelo and Busy Bee was standing next to Golden Hawk.

The sky over head was a deep blue and there was one lone cloud slowly moving toward the sun.

The cry of the eagle brought her attention to the moment.

She was grabbing for Little Otter even before he slipped on the snow-covered slope.

She had him by the hair.

She pulled him with all her might, took two steps backward and fell but held tight to Little Otter's hair.

The final part of Broken Spear message to her.

"If you do, you will have a long and prosperous time together," went through her mind as she struggled to get out from under Little Otter.

He was holding his head as she sat down beside him. He thanked her for saving his life. He knew that had he fallen into the trench he would have been trampled.

He put his arm around her and gave her a hug.

Talking Wren did not say a word. She was absorbing the fact that she had just met her lifetime mate.

High above the eagle let out a cry and flew away.

Talking Wren looked over at Taelo. He nodded his head in the same manner as Broken Spear.

She surmised that he had somehow known what was about to happen.

She looked up to the eagle that had spoken to her and knew that at the cave of the Others, Broken Spear would have watched and knew that she had listened to his words.

She spent the rest of the hunt and the travel back to the clan in a relatively quiet evaluation of her new understanding.

When Busy Bee and Quiet Rabbit asked if she was not feeling well, she laughed and replied that she was feeling better than she had ever felt.

She realized that she had drawn their attention because she had been talking a lot less.

Perhaps that was a good thing. She was in a place she had not expected to be, but she was where she knew she wanted to be.

The End

Thank you for reading this story.

About the Author

Ronald E. Mueller
remwriter95@gmail.com

Ron grew up in what is now Flint River State Park in Southeast Iowa. The 170-year-old house Ron lived in is built into a hillside. It faces a 125-foot-high cliff towering over the little Flint River. The house and the land talked to him about; the passing of time, the struggle to conquer the land, the struggles people faced and the wonder of nature.

He climbed the cliffs, crawled into the caves, dove from the swimming rock, collected clams from the bottom of the pond, gigged and skinned frogs for their legs. He trapped muskrats for fur, hunted raccoon in the dead of night, and with only a stick hunted rabbits in the dead of winter.

His young life was outdoors, and nature tested him.

He walked to a one room stone schoolhouse uphill both ways. A stern but warm-hearted teacher, Mrs. Henry was instrumental in shaping his character as she shepherded him from the fourth to the eighth grade.

It was a great way to grow up.

Ron graduated from Burlington, High School, went to Vietnam in the Navy. He graduated from The University of South Florida with a master's degree in engineering, worked for thirty eight years for Procter and Gamble, traveled around the world thirty times.

He has remained happily married for more than fifty years. His daughter and his two sons are all successful and his three grandchildren have all graduated.

His wife has humored and supported him as he became a full time professional story teller.

He has come to realize that he is, what is known as, a Cozy writer. Excitement and adventure but little guts and gore. His heroine or hero suffer a little but live happily ever after.

His experiences inter-twined with snippets of fantasy lend themselves to the adventures he leads the reader through.

Ron Mueller

Books by Ron Mueller
Fiction Series
The Taelo Series
The Early Years
The Golden Feather
Journey of Discovery
Dangerous Passage
Condor Clan Slingers
Circumvention
The Journey of Sages
Future Leaders Journey
Taelo Collection

A Taelo Story

White Swan and Quiet Pheasant
The Child's Name
Floating Cloud
Quiet Rabbit
Busy Bee
Little Otter & Talking Wren
Broken Spear
Burley Bear & Meadow Flower
Taelo Story Collection

The Alex Evercrest Series
The River Front
The Girl on The Grill
Missing
Maggot
Racist
Votive Candles
Windy City
Country Road
Pool of Blood
Sins of the Daughter
Body Parts
The Skull Collector
The Vanishing
The Shadow Fighter
Moonshine
Grief's Trajectory
The Magic Touch
Northern Lights
Alex Evercrest Heroine
Alex Evercrest Collection Two
New Direction
A Family Affair
Disruption
The St. Lebuinnus Church Murder

A Brian O'Neil Novel
Hawaiian Phoenix
Moon Curser
Death Broker

The Problem Solver Series
Solutions
Drug Lords
Border Crosser
The Problem Solver Collection

Ron Mueller

Science Fiction

The Savitar Series:
Journey's End
Savitar
Confluence
Savitar Series Collection

Bram Nielson Series
The Fold
The Message
Fold Wormhole
Negative Fold
Ripples in Time
Bram Nielson Collection

Single Science Fiction Books:
Current Past and Future
The Event
The Door
Viajante 7

https://www.remwriter95.net/

Published by: Around the World Publishing LLC.